the
NIGHT
bus

To Greg Thoon.

For a bad hair day.

ORCHARD BOOKS
96 Leonard Street
London EC2A 4XD
Orchard Books Australia
Unit 31/56 O'Riordan Street, Alexandria, NSW 2015
First published in Great Britain in two volumes as
Horowitz Horror in 1999 and *More Horowitz Horror* in 2000
This edition published in 2002
Text © Anthony Horowitz 1999
The right of Anthony Horowitz to be identified as the author
of this work has been asserted by him in accordance with
the Copyright, Designs and Patents Act, 1988.
A CIP catalogue record for this book is available from
the British Library.
1 3 5 7 9 10 8 6 4 2
ISBN 1 84121 372 1
Printed in Great Britain

the
NIGHT
bus

ANTHONY HOROWITZ

ORCHARD BOOKS

Contents

the
NIGHT
bus

Nick Hancock and his brother, Jeremy, knew they were in trouble but what they couldn't agree on was whose fault it was.

Jeremy blamed Nick, of course. Nick blamed Jonathan Saunders. And they both knew that when they finally got home – if they ever got home – their dad would blame them. But whoever was guilty, the fact was that they were stuck in the middle of London. It was five minutes to midnight. And they should have been home twenty-five minutes ago.

It was a Saturday night – and not just any Saturday night. This was October the 31st. Halloween. The two of them had been invited to a party in central London, just off Holborn. Even getting permission to go had been hard work. Nick was seventeen and was allowed out on his own. His younger brother, Jeremy, was just twelve although it was true that in another week he'd be a teenager himself. The party was being given by their cousin and that was what probably changed their parents' minds. Anybody else's party would be drugs, alcohol and vomit...at least, that was how they saw it. But this was family. How could they say no?

John Hancock, the boys' father, had finally agreed. 'All right,' he said. 'The two of you can go. But I want you home by half eleven...no arguments! Has Jonathan been invited?'

Jonathan Saunders lived just down the road. The three of them all went to the same school.

'Fine. I'll take the three of you. His mum or dad can bring you back. I'll give them a call. And Nick – you look after your brother. I just hope I'm not going to regret this...'

It had all gone horribly wrong. John Hancock had driven the three boys all the way into town. It was about a forty-minute journey from Richmond, where they all lived, out on the western edge of the city.

John, who worked as a copywriter in one of the main advertising agencies, usually took the tube. But how could he take three boys across London on public transport when one of them was dressed up as a devil, one as a vampire and the last (Jonathan) as Frankenstein, complete with a bolt going through his neck?

He had dropped them off at the house near Holborn and it had been a great party. The trouble came at the end of it, at eleven o'clock. Jonathan had said it was time to go. Nick and Jeremy had wanted to stay. And what with the noise of the music and the darkness and the crowds of other kids, they had somehow got their wires crossed.

Jonathan had left without them.

His mother, who had come to pick the three of them up, had cheerfully driven off into the night taking Jonathan but leaving the two other boys behind. Catherine Saunders was like that. She was a writer, a novelist who was always dreaming of her next plot. She was the sort of person who could drive to work only to find she'd forgotten the car. Scatty – that was her nickname. Maybe, at the end of the day, the blame was hers.

And this *was* the end of the day. It was five to twelve and Nick, dressed as the devil, and Jeremy, as Count Dracula, were feeling very small and stupid as they walked together through Trafalgar Square in the heart of London.

'We shouldn't have left,' Jeremy said, miserably.

'We had to. If Uncle Colin had seen us, he'd have called Dad and you know what that would have meant. Grounded for a month.'

'Instead of which we'll be grounded for a year...'

'We'll get home...'

'We should have been there twenty minutes ago!'

They should, of course, have taken a taxi – but there were no free taxis around. They had thought about the tube train. But somehow they'd missed Holborn and Covent Garden tube stations and had found themselves in Trafalgar Square, in the shadow of Nelson's Column, before they knew where they were. Surprisingly, there weren't that many people around. Perhaps it was too late for the theatregoers, who would already be well on their way home, and too early for the clubbers who wouldn't even think about home until dawn. A few people glanced in the boys' direction as they made their way round the stone lions that guarded the square but quickly looked away. After all, what do you say to Dracula and the devil at five to twelve on a Saturday night?

'What are we going to do?' Jeremy complained. It felt like he'd been walking for ever. He was cold and his feet were aching.

'The night bus!' Nick spoke the words even as he saw the bus in question, parked at the far corner of the square, opposite the National Gallery.

'Where?'

'There!'

Nick pointed and there it was, an old-fashioned red bus with a hop-on, hop-off platform at the back and the magical word RICHMOND printed in white letters on the panel above the driver's cabin. The bus was the 227B. Its other destinations were printed underneath: ST MARK'S GROVE, PALLISER ROAD, FULHAM PALACE ROAD, LOWER MILL HILL ROAD and CLIFFORD AVENUE. At least two of the names were familiar to Nick. The bus was heading west. And they had enough money for the fare.

'Come on!' Jeremy had already broken into a run, his vampire cloak billowing behind him. Nick tightened his grip on his pitchfork and ran after his younger brother, at the same time clinging on to his horns which were slipping off his head.

They reached the bus, climbed on, and took a seat about halfway along the lower deck. It was only when they were sitting down that Nick became aware that there were no lights on the bus, no other passengers, no driver and no conductor. With a sinking feeling he realised that this was one bus that wasn't going anywhere – at least not in the near future. Next to him, Jeremy was sitting back panting with his eyes half-closed. He looked at his watch. Eleven fifty-nine and counting. Ten seconds to midnight. Maybe it would be better to try again for a taxi, he decided. A taxi would have to drive through Trafalgar Square sooner or later.

'Jerry...' he said.

And, at the same moment, the lights came on, the

engine rumbled into life, the bell rang and the bus lurched forward.

Nick looked up, slightly alarmed. The bus had been empty a few seconds ago, he was sure of it. But now he could see the hunched-over shoulders and dark hair of a driver, sitting in the cabin. And there was a conductor on the platform, dressed in a crumpled grey uniform that looked at least ten years out of date, feeding a paper spool into his ticket machine.

Nick and Jeremy were still the only passengers.

'Jerry...?' he whispered.

'What?'

'Did you see the driver get on?'

'What driver?' Jeremy was half-asleep.

Nick looked out of the window as the bus turned up Haymarket and made its way towards Piccadilly Circus. They passed a second bus stop with a few people waiting but the night bus didn't stop. Nor did the people waiting seem to notice it going past. Nick felt the first prickles of unease. There was something dreamlike about this whole journey; the empty bus that wasn't stopping, the driver and conductor appearing out of nowhere, even Jeremy and himself, wearing these ridiculous costumes, travelling through London in the middle of the night.

The conductor walked up the bus towards them. 'Where to?' he demanded.

Now that Nick could see the man close to, he felt all the more uneasy. The conductor looked more dead than alive. His face was quite white, with sunken eyes and limp black hair hanging down. He was frighteningly thin. There seemed to be almost no flesh at all on his hands, which were clasped round the ticket machine; not one of the new-fangled ones that worked electronically but an old-fashioned thing with a wheel that you had to crank to spit the tickets out. But then the whole bus was completely out of date: the pattern on the seats, the shape of the windows, the cord suspended from the ceiling that you pulled to ring the bell, even the posters on the walls advertising products he had never heard of.

'Where to?' the conductor asked. He had a voice that seemed to echo before it had even left his mouth.

'Two to Richmond,' Nick said.

The conductor looked at him more closely. 'I haven't seen you before,' he said.

'Well...' Nick wasn't sure what to say. 'We don't go out this late very often.'

'You're very young,' the conductor said. He glanced at Jeremy who was now completely asleep. 'Is he your brother?'

'Yes.'

'So how did you both go?'

'I'm sorry?'

'How did you depart? What was it that...' the conductor coughed politely, '...took you?'

'My dad's car,' Nick replied, mystified.

'Tragic.' The conductor sighed and shook his head. 'So where are you going?'

'Richmond, please.'

'Lower Grove Road, I suppose. All right...' The conductor's hand rattled round in a circle and a double ticket jerked out of the machine. He handed it to Nick. 'That'll be a shilling.'

'I'm sorry?' Nick was mystified. He handed the conductor a one-pound coin and the man squinted at it distastefully. 'New currency,' he muttered. 'I still haven't got used to it. All right...' He reached into his pocket and pulled out a handful of change including several large pennies and even a threepenny piece. The last time Nick had seen one of those it had been in an antiques shop. But he didn't dare complain. Nor had he mentioned that they didn't actually want to go to Lower Grove Road. He didn't even know where it was. He didn't say anything. The bus driver walked back to the platform and left him on his own.

The bus drove round Hyde Park Corner, down through Knightsbridge and on through South Kensington. At least Nick recognised the roads and knew they were heading in the right direction. But the bus hadn't stopped; not once. Nobody had got on, not even when it was waiting at the red traffic light near Harrods. Jeremy was asleep, snoring lightly. Nick was sitting still, counting the minutes. He just wanted to be in Richmond. No matter how furious his parents would be when he finally arrived, he wanted to get back home.

And then, on the other side of Kensington, just past

the Virgin Cinema on the Fulham Road, the bus finally pulled in. 'St Mark's Grove,' the conductor called out. Nick looked out of the window. There was a tall, black, metal grille on the other side of the road and a sign that he couldn't quite read in the darkness. A group of people had been waiting just in front of it and as he watched they crossed over the road and got on to the bus. The conductor pulled the cord twice and they moved off again.

Four men and three women had got on. They were all extremely well dressed, and Nick assumed they must have all come from the same dinner party. Or perhaps they'd been to the opera. Two of the men were wearing black tie with wing collars. One also had a white scarf and an ebony walking-stick. The women were in long dresses, though they wore no jewellery. They were all fairly elderly, perhaps in their sixties – but then, just as the bus picked up speed, a fifth man suddenly ran to catch up with it, reached out a hand and pulled himself on to the moving platform. Nick gasped. This was a much younger man, a motor cyclist still dressed in his leathers and carrying his helmet. But at some time he must have been involved in a terrible accident. There was a livid scar running down the side of his face and part of his head had crumpled inwards like a punctured football. The man had staring eyes and a huge grin that had nothing to do with humour. The scar had wasted his flesh, pulling one side of his lip back to expose a row of heavy, yellowing teeth. He was also dirty and smelt; the sour smell of old, damp earth. Nick wanted to stare at him but he forced himself to look away. The motor cyclist plumped himself down on a seat a few places behind him. Looking out of the corner of his eye, Nick could just make out his reflection in the glass of the window.

Curiously, the smartly dressed people seemed quite happy to have the motor cyclist in their midst.

'You only just caught it!' one of them exclaimed, nodding at the bus.

'Yeah.' The other side of his mouth twitched and for a moment the smile on his face looked almost natural. 'I got up late.'

Got up late? Nick wondered what he meant. It

was, after all, a quarter past twelve at night.

'Seven tickets to Queensmill Road,' one of the women told the conductor. The handle cranked round four times, spitting out a length of white ticket.

'Queensmill Road!' the motor cyclist exclaimed. 'That's near where I had my accident.' He touched his wounded head with his finger although to Nick, watching all this in the reflection of the window, it looked as if he actually put his finger through the wound and *into* his head. 'I collided with a mobile library,' he explained.

'Did you get booked for bad driving?' the man with the silk scarf asked and the entire company roared with laughter at the joke.

The bus stopped for a second time about five minutes later.

'Palliser Road,' the conductor called out.

At least a dozen people were waiting at the stop and they had clearly all been to the same Halloween party. They were in a lively mood as they got on to the night bus, chatting among themselves and wearing a bizarre assortment of fancy-dress costumes. Nick couldn't help looking over his shoulder as they took the seats all around them. There were two women dressed in eerie, green robes like ghosts. There were two skeletons. A boy only a few years older than Nick himself, had a knife jutting out from between his shoulders and crimson blood trickling from the corner of his mouth. An older couple had chosen, for some reason, to wear Victorian dress complete with top hat and tails for the man and flowing ballgown for the woman. Although it wasn't raining outside, both of them were dripping wet. The man noticed Nick staring at him. 'Last time I take a holiday on the *Titanic*!' he exclaimed. Nick looked the other way, embarrassed.

The people from the first bus stop soon fell into conversation with the people from the second stop and the atmosphere on the bus became quite party-like itself.

'Sir Oswald! I haven't seen you for what...? Thirty years? You look terrible!'

'Barbara, isn't it? Barbara Bennett! How is your husband? Still alive? Oh – I am sorry to hear it.'

Yes, I took the family skiing for Christmas. We had a marvellous time except unfortunately I had a massive heart attack...'

'Actually, I'm popping down to Putney to see the Fergusons. Lovely couple. Both blown up in the war...'

This went on for the next half-hour. The other passengers ignored Nick and he was grateful for it. Although he was completely surrounded by them he felt somehow different to them. He couldn't quite explain how. Perhaps it was the fact that they all seemed to know each other. They just somehow had more in common.

The night bus stopped three more times. At Queensmill Road, where the seven party-goers got off. At Lower Mill Hill Road. And finally at Clifford Avenue. By the time it left this third stop, the bus was completely full, with people standing in the corridor and on the platform. The last person to get on was more peculiar than any of them. He seemed to have just escaped from a fire. His clothes were charred and in tatters. Smoke was drifting up from his armpits and he could only nod his head in apology as the conductor tapped him on the shoulder and pointed to the 'No Smoking' sign.

If anything, the party atmosphere had intensified. All around Nick there were people talking so loudly that he could no longer hear the engine while the passengers on the upper deck had broken into song, a chorus of 'John Brown's body lies a mould'ring in the grave' which seemed to cause them great merriment. Nick tried not to stare but he couldn't help himself. As the bus approached the shops on the outskirts of Richmond, a huge, fat woman dressed, bizarrely, in a green surgical gown and sitting next to a small, bald man, suddenly turned round and blinked at him.

'What are you looking at?' she demanded.

'I wasn't...' Nick was completely tongue-tied. 'I'm sorry. It's just that I'm very late. And my parents are going to kill me!'

'It's a bit late for that, isn't it?'

'I don't know what you mean.'

'Well that's your funeral. Your funeral!' The woman roared with laughter and nudged the bald man so hard that he fell off his seat.

Laughter echoed through the night bus. There was more singing upstairs. A man in a three-piece suit muttered a quiet 'Excuse me' and brushed a maggot off his knee. The woman next to him held a handkerchief to her nose while the woman behind her appeared to pull her nose off and hold it to her handkerchief.

Nick had had enough. The bus was approaching the centre of the town. He recognised the shops. It slowed down for a red light and that was when he decided. He grabbed hold of Jeremy, waking him up.

'Come on!' he hissed.

'What?'

'We're here!'

Half-dragging his brother, Nick got to his feet and began to push his way to the back of the bus. The light was still red but he knew it would change any second now. The other passengers didn't try to stop him, but they seemed surprised that he should be trying to get off.

'You can't leave here!' one of them exclaimed.

'We're not there yet!'

'What are you doing?'

'Come back!'

The light turned yellow, then green. The bus moved forward.

'Stop!'

'Stop him!'

The conductor, standing at the back of the platform, lunged towards Nick and for a second he felt fingers as cold as ice clamp round his arm. 'Jump!' he shouted. Jeremy jumped off the moving bus and Nick, clinging on to his brother with one hand, was pulled with him. The conductor cried out and released him. And then they were both sprawling on the road while the night bus thundered on, rattling down the high street and on into the shadows beyond.

'What was all that about?' Jeremy said, pulling himself to his feet.

'I don't know,' Nick muttered. He knelt where he was, watching as the night bus turned a corner and disappeared, a last chorus of 'John Brown' hanging like some invisible creature in the air before swooping away and racing after it.

'I've twisted my ankle,' Jeremy groaned.

'It doesn't matter.' Nick got up and went over to his brother. 'We're home.'

'You are the most irresponsible, disobedient, bloody children I've ever met! Do you realise I was two inches away from calling the police about you? Your mother and I were sick with worry. This is the last time you go to a party on your own. In fact it's the last time you go to any party at all! I can't believe you could be so stupid...'

It was Sunday morning, breakfast, and John Hancock was still in a rage. Of course he'd been waiting for the boys when they got home, cold and exhausted, at ten to one. That night he'd rationed himself to ten minutes' shouting but after a good night's sleep it seemed he was going to rage on until lunch. In his heart, Nicholas couldn't blame him. His parents had been scared – that was the truth of it. Admittedly he was seventeen and could look after himself, but Jeremy was just twelve. And there were lots of weirdos out on the streets. Everyone knew that.

Weirdos...

'I want you to tell me more about how you got home,' his mother said. Rosemary Hancock was a quiet, sensible woman who was used to stepping in between the father and his sons when arguments flared...which they often did in the small, crowded household. She managed a bookshop in Richmond and Nick noticed she had two books with her now. One was a history of London. The other was a map book. She had brought them to the table along with the croissants and coffee.

'They already told us,' John scowled.

Rosemary ignored him. 'You said you took the 227B bus,' she said. 'An old-fashioned bus. Did it look like this?' She showed Nicholas a photograph in the book. It showed a bus just like the one he had been on.

'What does it matter what the bus looked like?' John said.

'Yes. It was just like that,' Jeremy interrupted. 'With the open door at the back.'

'And the conductor gave you old coins?'

'Yes.' Nick had left the coins beside his bed. In the daylight they had looked more than old. Some of them were rusty and coated in some sort of slime. Just looking at them had made him shudder although he couldn't say quite why.

'Do you remember where the bus stopped?' Rosemary asked. She closed the book. 'You said it went to Clifford Avenue and Lower Mill Hill Road.'

'Yes.' Nick thought back. 'It stopped in Fulham first. St Peter's Grove or something. And then at Palliser Road. And then...'

'Would it have been Queensmill Road?' Rosemary asked.

Nick stared at her. 'Yes. How do you know?'

'What are you going on about?' John demanded. 'What does it matter what the bus looked like or where it went?'

'It's just that there is no 227B bus,' Rosemary replied. 'I rang London Transport this morning while you were out getting the croissants. There is a bus that goes from Trafalgar Square to Richmond but it's the N9.'

She tapped the book. 'And the bus that the boys described, the one I showed them in the photograph...it's an old Routemaster. They haven't built buses like that for thirty years and there certainly aren't any on the road.'

'Well then, how...?' John turned to look at Nick.

But Nick's eyes were fixed on his mother. The blood was draining from his face. He could actually feel it being sucked down his neck. 'But you knew the route,' he said.

'I don't know exactly what's going on here,' Rosemary began. 'Either you two boys have made the whole thing up or...I don't know...I suppose it must have been a practical joke or something.'

'Go on,' Nick said. He reached for his orange juice and took a sip. His mouth had gone dry.

'Well, it seems that last night you two did a tour of west London's cemeteries.' She opened the map book and pointed. 'St Mark's Grove, just off the Fulham Road...'

Nick remembered the tall metal grille and the sign.

'...that's Brompton Cemetery. Hammersmith

Cemetery is on Palliser Road. Fulham Cemetery…
that's on the Fulham Palace Road but it's opposite
Queensmill Road. Putney Cemetery is on Lower Mill Hill
Road and Clifford Avenue, where you say you saw
that man who seemed to be smouldering or on fire –
well, that's Mortlake Crematorium.'

She closed the book.

Jeremy was sitting in his seat, a piece of croissant
halfway to his lips.

John Hancock stood up. 'Of course it was a
practical joke,' he said. 'Now you'd better help me
get Nick off the floor. He seems to have fainted.'

the
HITCHHIKER

Why
did
my father
have
to
stop?

I told him not to. I knew it was a bad idea. Of course, he didn't listen to me. Parents never do. But it would never have happened if only he'd driven on.

We'd been out for the day, just the three of us, and what a great, really happy day it had been. My fifteenth birthday, and they had taken me to Southwold, a small town on the Suffolk coast. We'd got there just in time for lunch and had spent the afternoon walking on the beach, looking in the shops and losing money in the crummy arcade down by the pier.

A lot of people would think that Southwold was a rubbish place to go, especially on your birthday. But they'd be wrong. The truth is that it's special. From the multicoloured beach huts that have probably been there since Queen Victoria's time, to the cannons on the cliff which have certainly been there a whole lot longer. It's got a lighthouse and a brewery and a sloping village green that all look as if they've come out of an Enid Blyton story. None of the shops seem to sell anything that anyone would actually want and there's one, in the High Street, that has these fantastic wooden toys. A whole circus that comes to life for twenty pence. And the talking head of Horatio Nelson who puts his telescope up to his missing eye and sings. You get real fish and chips in Southwold. Fish that were still swimming while you were driving to the restaurant. Sticky puddings with custard. I don't need to go on. The whole place is so old-fashioned and so English that it just makes you want to smile.

We started back at about five o'clock. There was a real Suffolk sunset that evening. The sky was pink and grey and dark blue and somehow there was almost too much of it. I sat in the back of the car and as the door slammed I felt that strange, heavy feeling you get at the end of a really good day. I was sad that it was over. But I felt happy and tired, glad that it was over too.

It was only about an hour's drive and as we left

Southwold it began to rain. There's nothing strange about that. The weather often changes rapidly in Suffolk. By the time we reached the A12, the rain was falling quite heavily, slanting down, grey needles in the breeze. And there, ahead of us on the road, was a man, walking quickly, his hands clenched on the sides of his jacket, pulling it around him. He didn't turn round as we approached but he must have heard us coming. Suddenly his hand shot out. One thumb jutted out; the universal symbol of the hitchhiker. He wanted a lift.

There were about fifteen seconds until we reached him. My father was the first to speak.

'I wonder where he's going.'

'You're not going to stop,' my mother said.

'Why not? It's a horrible evening. Look at the weather!'

And there you have my parents. My father is a dentist and maybe that's why he's always trying to be nice to people. He knows that nobody in their right mind really wants to see him. He's tall and shambolic, the sort of man who goes to work with his hair unbrushed and with socks that don't match. My mother works three days a week at an estate agency. She's much tougher than him. When I was young, she was always the one who would send me to bed. He'd let me stay up all night if she wasn't there.

There's one more thing I have to tell you about them. They both look quite a bit older than they actually are. There's a reason for this. My older brother, Eddy. He died suddenly when he was twelve years old. That was nine years ago and my parents have never really recovered. I miss him too. Of course, he bullied me sometimes like all big brothers do, but his death was a terrible thing. It hurt us all and we know that the pain will never go away.

Anyway, it was typical of my dad to want to stop and offer the man a lift and just as typical of my mum to want to drive on. In the back seat, I said, 'Don't stop, Dad.' But it was already too late. Just fifteen seconds had passed since we saw the hitchhiker and already we were slowing down. I'd told him not to stop. But I'd no sooner said it than we did.

The rain was coming down harder now and it was

very dark so I couldn't see very much of the man. He seemed quite large, towering over the car. He had long hair, hanging down over his eyes.

My father pressed the button that lowered the window. 'Where are you going?' he asked.

'Ipswich.'

Ipswich was about twenty miles away. My mother didn't say anything. I could tell she was uncomfortable.

'You were heading there on foot?' my father asked.

'My car's broken down.'

'Well – we're heading that way. We can give you a lift.'

'John...' My mother spoke my father's name quietly but already it was too late. The damage was done.

'Thanks,' the man said. He opened the back door.

I suppose I'd better explain.

The A12 is a long, dark, anonymous road that often goes through empty countryside with no buildings in sight. It was like that where we were now. There were no street lights. Pulled in on the hard shoulder, we must have been practically invisible to the other traffic rushing past. It was the one place in the world where you'd have to be crazy to pick up a stranger.

Because, you see, everyone knows about Fairfields. It's a big, ugly building not far from Woodbridge, surrounded by a wall that's fifteen metres high with spikes along the top and metal gates that open electrically. The name is quite new. It used to be called the East Suffolk Maximum Security Prison for the Criminally Insane. And right now we were only about ten miles away from it.

That's the point I'm trying to make. When you're ten miles away from a lunatic asylum, you don't stop in the dark to pick up someone you've never met. You have to say to yourself that maybe, just maybe, there could have been a break-out that night. Maybe one of the loonies has cut the throat of the guard at the gate and slipped out into the night. And so it doesn't matter if it's raining. It doesn't even matter if the local nuclear power station at Sizewell has just blown up and it's coming down radioactive slush. You just don't stop.

The back door slammed shut. The man eased

himself into the back seat, rain water glistening on his jacket. The car drove forward again.

I looked at him, trying to make out his features in the half light. He had a long face with a square chin and small, narrow eyes. His skin was pale, as if he hadn't been outdoors in a while. His hair was somewhere between brown and grey, hanging down in clumps. His clothes looked old and second-hand. A sports jacket and baggy corduroys. The sort of clothes a gardener might wear. His fingers were unusually long. One hand was resting on his thigh and his fingers reached all the way to his knee.

'Have you been out for the day?' he asked.

'Yes.' My father knew he had annoyed my mother and he was determined to be cheerful and chatty, to show that he wasn't ashamed of what he'd done. 'We've been in Southwold. It's a beautiful place.'

'Oh yes.' He glanced at me and I saw that he had a scar running over his eye. It began on his forehead and ended on his cheek and it seemed to have pushed the eye a little to one side. It wasn't quite level with the other one.

'Do you know Southwold?' my father asked.

'No.'

'So where have you come from today?'

The man thought for a moment. 'I broke down near Lowestoft,' he said and somehow I knew he was lying. For a start, Lowestoft was a long way away, right on the border with Norfolk. If he'd broken down there, how could he have managed to get all the way to Southwold? And why bother? It would have been easier to jump on a train and go straight to Ipswich. I opened my mouth to say something but the man looked at me again, more sharply this time. Maybe I was imagining it but he could have been warning me. Don't say anything. Don't ask any difficult questions.

'What's your name?' my mother asked. I don't know why she wanted to know.

'Rellik,' he said. 'Ian Rellik.' He smiled slowly. 'This your son in the back?'

'Yes. That's Jacob. He's fifteen today.'

'His birthday?' The man uncurled his hand and held it out to me. 'Happy birthday, Jacob.'

'Thank you.' I took the hand. It was like holding a dead fish. At the same time I glanced down and saw that his sleeve had pulled back exposing his wrist. There was something glistening on his skin and it wasn't rain water. It was dark red, trickling down all the way to the edge of his hand, rising over the fleshy part of his thumb.

Blood!

Whose blood? His own?

He pulled his hand away, hiding it behind him. He knew I had seen it. Maybe he wanted me to.

We drove on. A cloud must have burst because it was really lashing down. You could hear the rain thumping on the car roof and the windscreen wipers were having to work hard to sweep it aside. I couldn't believe we'd been walking on the beach only a few hours before.

'Lucky we got in,' my mother said, reading my mind.

'It's bad,' my father said.

'It's hell,' the man muttered. Hell. It was a strange choice of word. He shifted in his seat. 'What do you do?' he asked.

'I'm a dentist.'

'Really? I haven't seen a dentist...not for a long time.' He ran his tongue over his teeth. The tongue was pink and wet. The teeth were yellow and uneven. I guessed he hadn't cleaned them in a while.

'You should go twice a year,' my father said.

'You're right. I should.'

There was a rumble of thunder and at that exact moment the man turned to me and mouthed two words. He didn't say them. He just mouthed them, making sure my parents couldn't see.

'*You're dead.*'

I stared at him, completely shaken. At first I thought I must have misunderstood him. Maybe he had said something else and the words had got lost in the thunderclap. But then he nodded slowly, telling me that I wasn't wrong. That's what he'd said. And that's what he meant.

I felt every bone in my body turn to jelly. That thing about the asylum. When we'd stopped and picked up the hitchhiker, I hadn't *really* believed that he was a madman who'd just escaped. Often you get scared by things but you can still tell yourself that it's just your imagination, that you're being stupid. And after all, there are lots of stories about escaped lunatics and none of them are ever true. But now I wasn't so sure. Had I imagined it? Had he said something else? *You're dead.* I thought back, picturing the movement of his lips. He'd said it all right.

We were doing about forty miles per hour, punching through the rain. I turned away, trying to ignore the man on the seat beside me. Mr Rellik. There was something strange about that name and without really thinking I found myself writing it on the window, using the tip of my finger.

RELLIK

The letters, formed out of the condensation inside the car, hung there for a moment. Then the two `l's in the middle began to run. It reminded me of blood. The name sounded Hungarian or something. It made me think of someone in *Dracula*.

'Where do you want us to drop you?' my mother asked.

'Anywhere,' Mr Rellik said.

'Where do you live in Ipswich?'

There was a pause. 'Blade Street,' he said.

'Blade Street? I don't think I know it.'

'It's near the centre.'

My mother knew every street in Ipswich. She lived there for ten years before she married my father. But she had never heard of Blade Street. And why had the hitchhiker paused before he answered her question? Had he been making it up?

The thunder rolled over us a second time.

'*I'm going to kill you*,' Mr Rellik said.

But he said it so quietly that only I heard and this time I knew for certain. He was mad. He had escaped from Fairfields. We had picked him up in the middle of nowhere and he was going to kill us all. I leant forward, trying to catch my parents' eyes. And that was when I happened to look into the driver's mirror. That was when I saw the word that I had written on the window just a few moments before.

RELLIK

But reflected in the mirror it said something else.

KILLER

What was I supposed to do? What would you do if you were in my situation? We were still doing forty miles an hour in the rain, following a long empty road with fields on one side, trees on the other and thick darkness everywhere. We were trapped inside the car with a man who could have a knife on him or even a gun or something worse. My parents didn't know anything but for some reason the man had made himself known to me. So what were my choices?

I could scream.

He would lash out and stop me before I had even opened my mouth. I could imagine those long fingers closing on my throat. He would strangle me in the back seat and my parents would drive on without even knowing what had happened. Until it was their turn.

I could trick him.

I could say I was feeling car sick. I could make them stop the car and then, when we got out, I could somehow persuade my parents to run for it. But that was a bad idea too. We were safer while we were still moving. At least Mr Rellik – or whatever his real name was – couldn't attack my father while he was driving. The car would go out of control. He couldn't reach my mother either. That would mean lunging diagonally across the car and somehow getting over the back of her seat. No. I was the only one in danger right now…but that would change the moment we stopped.

Could I talk to him? Reason with him? Hope against hope that I had imagined it all and that he didn't mean us any harm?

And then I remembered.

I was sitting behind my mother for a reason. When we had set out that morning my father had told me to sit there because there was something wrong with the door on the other side. It was an old car, a

Volkswagen Estate, and the catch on one of the passenger doors had broken. My mother had said it was dangerous and had told me to sit on the left hand side and to be sure that I wore my seatbelt. I was wearing it now. But Mr Rellik wasn't.

I shifted round in my seat as if trying to get more comfortable. Mr Rellik was instantly alert. I could see that if I was going to try something I would have to move fast. He had told me who he was. He knew that I knew. He was almost expecting me to try something.

'We'll drop you off at the next roundabout,' my father said.

'That'll be fine.' But the hitchhiker had no intention of getting out at the next roundabout. His face darkened. The eye with the scar twitched. As I watched, his hand slid into his jacket and curled round something underneath the material. I didn't have to see it to know what it was. A knife. A moment later his hand reappeared and I caught the glint of silver. I knew exactly what was going to happen. He would attack me. My father would stop the car. What else could he do? Then it would be his turn. And then my mother's.

I yelled out. And then everything happened in a blur.

I had already got myself into position, curled up in the corner with my shoulders pressed into the side of the car to give me leverage. At the same time, my legs shot out. Mr Rellik had made a bad mistake. With his hand underneath his jacket he couldn't defend himself. Both my feet slammed into him, one on his shoulder, one just above his waist. I had kicked him with all my strength and as my legs uncoiled he was thrown against the opposite door.

The catch gave way. Mr Rellik didn't even have time to cry out. The door swung open and he was thrown out. Out into the night and the rain. My father must have speeded up without my noticing because we were doing almost sixty then and it seemed that the wind plucked Mr Rellik away. He hit the road in a spinning, splattering somersault. And it was worse than that. Although I hadn't seen it, an articulated lorry had been coming the other way, doing about the same speed as us. Mr Rellik fell under its front wheels. The lorry made mincemeat of him.

My mother screamed. My father stopped the car.

The articulated lorry stopped.

Suddenly everything was silent apart from the rain hammering on the roof.

My father twisted round and stared at me. The side door was still hanging open. 'What...?' he began.

Quickly I explained. I told him everything. The name on the window. The lies Mr Rellik had told. The things he had said to me. The blood on his hand. The knife. My mother was in total shock. Her face was white and she was crying quietly. My father waited until I had finished, then he reached out and laid a hand on my arm. 'It's all right, Jacob,' he said. 'Wait here.'

He got out of the car and walked up the road. I could see him out of the back window. The lorry driver had stopped on the hard shoulder and the two of them met. There was no sign of Mr Rellik. He must have been spread out over a fair bit of the A12. It had been horrible, what had happened, but I wasn't afraid any more. I had done what I'd had to do. I'd saved both my parents and myself. We should never have stopped.

My father and the lorry driver talked for a few minutes. Then my father walked back to the car. The rain had eased off a little but he was still soaking wet.

'He's going to call the police,' my father said. 'We're nearly there so I said we'd go on. He's going to give our details to the police.'

'Did you tell him what happened?' I asked.

'Yes.' My father got back in behind the steering wheel. My mother was still crying. 'He knows you did the right thing, Jacob. Don't worry. We're going to leave now.'

We drove for another ten minutes and then, just past the first sign for Woodbridge, we turned off down a narrow lane. It twisted through woodland for about a mile and then we came to a high brick wall with spikes set along the top. We stopped in front of a pair of metal gates with an intercom system just in front. My father leant out of the car window and said something. The gates clicked and swung open automatically.

I knew where we were. We had come to Fairfields. The East Suffolk Maximum Security Hospital for the Criminally Insane.

My father had to tell them what had happened, of course. He'd agreed that with the lorry driver. This is where Mr Rellik had come from and we had just killed him. In self defence. They had to know.

I asked my father if that was why we had come here.

'Yes, Jacob,' he said. 'That's why we're here.'

We drove towards a big Victorian house with towers and barred windows and blood-red bricks. I could see how the place had got its new name though. It was surrounded by attractive gardens, the lawns spreading out for some distance underneath the high voltage searchlights. Before we had even stopped, the front door of the house opened and a bald, bearded man in a white coat came running out.

'Wait here,' my father said again.

I waited with my mother while the two of them spoke but this time I managed to hear a little of what they said. My father did most of the talking.

'You were wrong, Dr Fielding. You were wrong. We should never have taken him…'

'None of us could have known. He was doing so well.'

'He was fine in Southwold. He was fine. I thought he was…normal. But then…this!'

'I don't know what to say to you, Mr Fisher. I don't…'

'Never again, Dr Fielding. For God's sake! Never again.'

The two men came to the car. My father leant in. 'We're going in with Dr Fielding,' he said.

'All right,' I said.

My mother didn't look up as I got out of the car. She didn't even say goodbye. That made me a little sad.

Dr Fielding put a hand on my shoulder. 'Let's go inside, Jacob,' he said. 'We have to talk about what happened.'

'All right,' I said.

Later on, they told me that the hitchhiker's name was Mr Renwick and that I had misheard him. Apparently Mr Renwick was a gardener who had been working outside Lowestoft. His car had broken down and he had managed to hitchhike as far as Southwold which was where we'd picked him up. They told me that it was mud I had seen on his wrist, not blood. And that when they had scraped him off the tarmac he had been holding not a knife but a cigarette case.

That was what they told me, but I didn't believe any of it. After all, they also told me a lot of lies after my brother Eddy fell under that train. They even wanted me to believe that I'd pushed him! Nobody ever understood.

So here I am, back in my room, looking out of the barred window at the same old view. I had such a nice day in Southwold. I just hope I won't have to wait another nine years before they take me out again.

the

man

with the

YELLOW

face

I
want
to tell you
how
it
happened.
But it's not easy. It's all a long time ago now and even though I think about it often, there are still things I don't understand. Maybe I never did.

Why did I even go into the machine? What I'm talking about is one of those instant photograph booths. It was on Platform One at York station – four shots for £2.50. It's probably still there now if you want to go and look at it. I've never been back so I can't be sure. Anyway, there I was with my uncle and aunt, waiting for the train to London and we were twenty minutes early and I had about three pounds on me, which was all that was left of my pocket money. I could have gone back to the kiosk and bought a comic, another bar of chocolate, a puzzle book. I could have gone into the café and bought Cokes all round. I could have just hung on to it. But maybe you know the feeling when you've been on holiday and your mum has given you a certain amount to spend. You've just got to spend it. It's almost a challenge. It doesn't matter what you spend it on. You've just got to be sure it's all gone by the time you get home.

Why the photographs? I was thirteen years old then and I suppose I was what you'd call good-looking. Girls said so, anyway. Fair hair, blue eyes, not fat, not thin. It was important to me how I looked – the right jeans, the right trainers, that sort of thing. But it wasn't crucial to me. What I'm trying to say is, I didn't take the photographs to pin on the wall or to prove to anyone what a movie star I was.

I just took them.

I don't know why.

It was the end of a long weekend in York. I was with my uncle and aunt because, back in London, my mum and dad were quietly and efficiently arranging their divorce. It was something that had been coming for a long time and I wasn't bothered by it any more but even so they'd figured it would upset me to see the removal men come in. My father was moving out of the house and into a flat and although my mother was keeping most of the furniture, there was still *his* piano, *his* books and pictures, *his* computer and the old wardrobe that he had inherited from *his* mother. Suddenly everything was his or hers. Before it had simply been ours.

Uncle Peter and Aunt Anne had been drafted in to keep me diverted while it all happened and they'd chosen York, I suppose, because it was far away and I'd never been there before. But if it was a diversion, it didn't really work. Because while I was in York Minster or walking around the walls or being trundled through the darkness in the Viking Museum, all I could think about was my father and how different everything would be without him, without the smell of his cigarettes and the sound of the out-of-tune piano echoing up the stairs.

I was spoiled that weekend. Of course, that's something parents do. The guiltier they feel, the more they'll spend and a divorce, the complete upheaval of my life and theirs, was worth plenty. I had twenty pounds to spend. We stayed in a hotel, not a bed and breakfast. Whatever I wanted, I got.

Even four useless photographs of myself from the photo booth on Platform One.

Was there something strange about that photo booth? It's easy enough to think that now but maybe even then I was a little...scared. If you've been to York you'll know that it's got a proper, old station with a soaring roof, steel girders and solid red brickwork. The platforms are long and curve round, following the rails. When you stand there you almost imagine that a steam train will pull in. A ghost train, perhaps. York is both a medieval and a Victorian city; enough ghosts for everyone.

But the photo booth was modern. It was an ugly metal box with its bright light glowing behind the plastic facings. It looked out-of-place on the platform – almost as if it had landed there from outer space. It was in a strange position too, quite a long way from the entrance and the benches where my uncle and aunt were sitting. You wouldn't have thought that many people would have come to this part of the platform. As I approached it, I was suddenly alone.

And maybe I imagined it but it seemed that a sudden wind had sprung up, as if blown my way by an approaching train. I felt the wind, cold against my face. But there was no train.

For a moment I stood outside the photo booth, wondering what I was going to do. One shot for the front of my exercise book. A shot for my father – he'd be seeing more of it now than he would of me. A silly, cross-eyed shot for the fridge... Somewhere behind me, the tannoy system sprang to life.

'The train now approaching Platform Two is the ten forty-five to Glasgow calling at Darlington, Durham, Newcastle...'

The voice sounded far away. Not even in the station. It was like a rumble coming out of the sky.

I pulled back the curtain and went into the photo booth.

There was a circular stool which you could adjust for height and a choice of backgrounds – a white curtain, a black curtain, or a blue wall. The people who designed these things were certainly imaginative. I sat down and looked at myself in the square of black glass in front of me. This was where the camera was, but looking in the glass I could only vaguely see my face. I could make out an outline; my hair falling down over one eye, my shoulders, the open neck of my shirt. But my reflection was shadowy and, like the voice on the tannoy, distant. It didn't look like me.

It looked more like my ghost.

Did I hesitate then, before I put the money in? I think I did. I didn't want these photographs. I was wasting my money. But at the same time I was here now and I might as well do it. I felt hemmed in, inside the photo booth, even though there was only one flimsy curtain separating me from the platform. Also, I was nervous that I was going to miss the train even though there were still fifteen minutes until it arrived. Suddenly I wanted to get it over with.

I put in the coins.

For a moment nothing happened and I thought the photo booth might be broken. But then a red light glowed somewhere behind the glass, deep inside the machine. A devil eye, winking at me. The light went out and there was a flash accompanied by a soft, popping sound that went right through my head.

The first picture had caught me unawares. I was just sitting there with my mouth half-open. Before the machine flashed again I quickly adjusted the stool and twisted my features into the most stupid face I could make. The red eye blinked, followed by the flash. That one would be for the fridge. For the third picture, I whipped the black curtain across, leant back and smiled. The picture was for my father and I wanted it to be good. The fourth picture was a complete disaster. I was pulling back the curtain, adjusting the stool and trying to think of something to do when the flash went off and I realised I'd taken a picture of my left shoulder with my face – annoyed and surprised – peering over the top.

That was it. Those were the four pictures I took.

I went outside the photo booth and stood there on my own, waiting for the pictures to develop. Three minutes according to the advert on the side. Nobody came anywhere near and once again I wondered why they had put the machine so far from the station entrance. Further up the platform, the station clock ticked to 10:47. The minute hand was so big that I could actually see it moving, sliding over the Roman numerals. Doors slammed on the other side of a train. There was the blast of a whistle. The 10:45 to Glasgow shuddered out of the station, a couple of minutes late.

The three minutes took an age to pass. Time always slows down when you're waiting for something. I watched the minute hand of the clock make two more complete circles. Another train, without any carriages, chugged backwards along a line on the far side of the station. And meanwhile the photo booth did...nothing. Maybe there were wheels turning inside, chemicals splashing, spools of paper unfolding. But from where I was standing it just looked dead.

Then, with no warning at all, there was a whirr and a strip of white paper was spat out of a slot in the side. My photographs. I waited until a fan had blown the paper dry, then prised it out of its metal cage. Being careful not to get my fingers on the pictures themselves, I turned them over in my hand.

Four pictures.

The first. Me looking stupid.

The second. Me out of focus.

The fourth. Me from behind.

But the third picture, in the middle of the strip, wasn't a picture of me at all.

It was a picture of a man, and one of the ugliest men I had ever seen. Just looking at him, holding him in my hand, sent a shiver all the way up my arm and round the back of my neck. The man had a yellow face. There was something terribly wrong with his skin which seemed to be crumpled up around his neck and chin, like an old paper bag. He had blue eyes but they had sunk back, hiding in the dark shadows of his eye sockets. His hair was grey and string-like, hanging lifelessly over his forehead. The skin here was damaged too, as if someone had drawn a map on it and then rubbed it out, leaving just faint traces. The man was leaning back against the black curtain and maybe he was smiling. His lips were certainly stretched in something like a smile but there was no humour there at all. He was staring at me, staring up from the palm of my hand. And I would have said his face was filled with raw horror.

I almost crumpled up the photographs then and there. There was something so shocking about the man that I couldn't bear to look at him. I tried to look at the three images of myself but each time my eyes were drawn down or up so that they settled only on him. I closed my fingers, bending them over his face, trying to blot him out. But it was too late. Even when I wasn't looking at him I could still see him. I could still feel him looking at me.

But who was he and how had he got there? I walked away from the machine, glad to be going back to where there were people, away from that deserted end of the platform. Obviously the photo booth *had* been broken. It must have muddled up my photographs with those of whoever had visited it just before me. At least, that's what I tried to tell myself.

My Uncle Peter was waiting for me at the bench. He seemed relieved to see me.

'I thought we were going to miss the train,' he said. He ground out the Gauloise he'd been smoking. He was as bad as my father when it came to cigarettes.

High-tar French. Not just damaging your health. Destroying it.

'So let's see them,' Aunt Anne said. She was a pretty, rather nervous woman who always managed to sound enthusiastic about everything. 'How did they come out?'

'The machine was broken,' I said.

'The camera probably cracked when it saw your face.' Peter gave one of his throaty laughs. 'Let's see...'

I held out the strip of film. They took it.

'Who's this?' Anne tried to sound cheerful but I could see that the man with the yellow face had disturbed her. I wasn't surprised. He'd disturbed me.

'He wasn't there,' I said. 'I mean, I didn't see him. All the photographs were of me – but when they were developed, he was there.'

'It must have been broken,' Peter said. 'This must be the last person who was in there.'

Which was exactly what I had thought. Only now I wasn't so sure. Because it had occurred to me that if there was something wrong with the machine and everyone was getting photographs of someone else, then surely the man with the yellow face would have appeared at the very top of the row: one photograph of him followed by three of me. Then whoever went in next would get one picture of me followed by three of them. And so on.

And there was something else.

Now that I thought about it, the man was sitting in exactly the same position that I'd taken inside the photo booth. I'd pulled the black curtain across for the third photograph and there it was now. I'd been leaning back and so was he. It was almost as if the man had somehow got into the machine and sat in a deliberate parody of me. And maybe there was something in that smile of his that was mocking and ugly. It was as if he were trying to tell me something. But I didn't want to know.

'I think he's a ghost,' I said.

'A ghost?' Peter laughed again. He had an annoying laugh. It was loud and jagged, like machine-gun fire. 'A ghost in a platform photo booth?'

'Peter...!' Anne was disapproving. She was worried about me. She'd been worried about me since the start of the divorce.

'I feel I know him,' I said. 'I can't explain it. But I've seen him somewhere before.'

'Where?' Anne asked.

'I don't know.'

'In a nightmare?' Peter suggested. 'His face does look a bit of a nightmare.'

I looked at the picture again even though I didn't want to. It was true. He did look familiar. But at the same time I knew that despite what I'd just said, it was a face I'd never seen before.

'The train now arriving at Platform One...'

It was the train announcer's voice again and sure enough there was our train, looking huge and somehow menacing as it slid round the curve of the track. And it was at that very moment, as I reached out to take the photographs, that I had the idea that I shouldn't get on the train because the man with the yellow face was going to be on it, that somehow he was dangerous to me and that the machine had sent me his picture to warn me.

My uncle and aunt gathered up our weekend bags.

'Why don't we wait?' I said.

'What?' My uncle was already halfway through the door.

'Can't we stay a little longer? In York? We could take the train this afternoon...'

'We've got to get back,' my aunt said. As always, hers was the voice of reason. 'Your mother's going to be waiting for us at the station and anyway, we've got reserved seats.'

'Come on!' Uncle Peter was caught between the platform and the train and with people milling around us, trying to get in, this obviously wasn't the best time or place for an argument.

Even now I wonder why I allowed myself to be pushed, or persuaded, into the train. I could have turned round and run away. I could have sat on the platform and refused to move. Maybe if it had been my mother and father there, I would have done but then, of course, if my mother and father had only managed to stay together in the first place none of it would have happened. Do I blame them? Yes. Sometimes I do.

I found myself on the train before I knew it. We had seats quite near the front and that also played a part in what happened. While Uncle Peter stowed the cases up on the rack and Aunt Anne fished in her shopping bag for magazines, drinks and sandwiches, I took the seat next to the window, miserable and afraid without knowing why.

The man with the yellow face. Who was he? A psychopath perhaps, released from a mental hospital, travelling to London with a knife in his raincoat pocket. Or a terrorist with a bomb, one of those suicide bombers you read about in the Middle East. Or a child killer. Or some sort of monster…

I was so certain I was going to meet him that I barely even noticed as the train jerked forward and began to move out of the station. The photographs were still clasped in my hand and I kept on looking from the yellow face to the other passengers in the carriage, expecting at any moment to see him coming towards me.

'What's the matter with you?' my uncle asked. 'You look like you've seen a ghost.'

I was expecting to. I said nothing.

'Is it that photograph?' Anne asked. 'Really, Simon, I don't know why it's upset you so much.'

And then the ticket collector came. Not a yellow face at all but a black one, smiling. Everything was normal. We were on a train heading for London and I had allowed myself to get flustered about nothing. I took the strip of photographs and bent it so that the yellow face disappeared behind the folds. When I got back to London, I'd cut it out. When I got back to London.

But I didn't get back to London. Not for a long, long time.

I didn't even know anything was wrong until it had happened. We were travelling fast, whizzing through green fields and clumps of woodland when I felt a slight lurch as if invisible arms had reached down and pulled me out of my seat. That was all there was at first, a sort of mechanical hiccup. But then I had the strange sensation that the train was flying. It was like a plane at the end of the runway, the front of the train separating from the ground. It could only have lasted a couple of seconds but in my memory those seconds seem to stretch out for ever. I remember my uncle's head turning, the question forming itself on his face. And my aunt, perhaps realising what was happening before we did, opening her mouth to scream. I remember the other passengers; I carry snapshots of them in my head. A mother with two small daughters, both with ribbons in their hair. A man with a moustache, his pen hovering over the *Times* crossword. A boy of about my own age, listening to a Walkman. The train was almost full. There was hardly an empty seat in sight.

And then the smash of the impact, the world spinning upside down, windows shattering, coats and suitcases tumbling down, sheets of paper whipping into my face, thousands of tiny fragments of glass swarming into me, the deafening scream of tearing metal, the sparks and the smoke and the flames leaping up, cold air rushing in and then the horrible rolling and shuddering that was like the very worst sort of fairground ride only this time the terror wasn't going to stop, this time it was all for real.

Silence.

They always say there's silence after an accident and they're right. I was on my back with something pressing down on me. I could only see out of one eye. Something dripped on to my face. Blood.

Then the screams began.

It turned out that some kids – maniacs – had dropped a concrete pile off a bridge outside Grantham. The train hit it and derailed. Nine people were killed in the crash and a further twenty-nine were seriously injured. I was one of the worst of them. I don't remember anything more of what happened, which is just as well as my carriage caught fire and I was badly burned before my uncle managed to drag me to safety. He was hardly hurt in the accident, apart from a few cuts and bruises. Aunt Anne broke her arm.

I spent many weeks in hospital and I don't remember much of that either. All in all, it was six months before I was better but 'better' in my case was never what I had been before.

This all happened thirty years ago.

And now?

I suppose I can't complain. After all, I wasn't killed and despite my injuries, I enjoy my life. But the injuries are still there. The plastic surgeons did what they could but I'd suffered third-degree burns over much of my body and there wasn't a whole lot they could do. My hair grew back but it's always been grey and rather lifeless. My eyes are sunken. And then there's my skin.

I sit here looking in the mirror.

And the man with the yellow face looks back.

More Orchard Black Apples

Orchard Black Apples are available from all good bookshops,
or can be ordered direct from the publisher:
Orchard Books, PO BOX 29, Douglas IM99 1BQ
Credit card orders please telephone 01624 836000
or fax 01624 837033
or e-mail: bookshop@enterprise.net for details.

To order please quote title, author and ISBN
and your full name and address.
Cheques and postal orders should be made payable to 'Bookpost plc.'
Postage and packing is FREE within the UK
(overseas customers should add £1.00 per book).

Prices and availability are subject to change.